W9-BQS-982

SUPER TURBO

PROTECTS THE WORLD

By Lee Kirby

Illustrated by George O'Connor

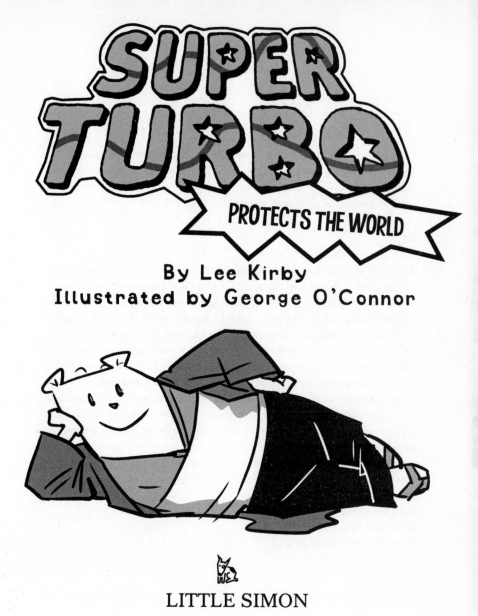

LITTLE SIMON

New York London Toronto Sydney New Delhi

LITTLE SIMON

An imprint of Simon & Schuster Children's Publishing Division • 1230 Avenue of the Americas, New York, New York 10020 • First Little Simon hardcover edition October 2017. Copyright © 2017 by Simon & Schuster, Inc. All rights reserved, including the right of reproduction in whole or in part in any form. LITTLE SIMON is a registered trademark of Simon & Schuster, Inc., and associated colophon is a trademark of Simon & Schuster, Inc. For information about special discounts for bulk purchases, please contact Simon & Schuster Special Sales at 1-866-506-1949 or business@simonandschuster.com. The Simon & Schuster Speakers Bureau can bring authors to your live event. For more information or to book an event contact the Simon & Schuster Speakers Bureau at 1-866-248-3049 or visit our website at www.simonspeakers.com. Designed by Jay Colvin. The text of this book was set in Little Simon Gazette.

Manufactured in the United States of America 0917 FFG 10 9 8 7 6 5 4 3 2 1

Cataloging-in-Publication Data for this title is available from the Library of Congress.

ISBN 978-1-4814-9994-1 (hc)

ISBN 978-1-4814-9993-4 (pbk)

ISBN 978-1-4814-9995-8 (eBook)

CONTENTS

1

IS IT HOT IN HERE?

BEHOLD! SUNNYVIEW ELEMENTARY SCHOOL!
INSIDE THESE WALLS, UH . . .

Wait, where are we? Are we even inside the walls of Sunnyview Elementary School?

Turbo the hamster, official pet of Classroom C, lay on his belly. Sweat dripped from his furry forehead. Heat beat down from above, and even seemed to be rising from the ground itself. Around him, all Turbo could see was yellow sand.

Turbo squinted in the bright light. Wavy images seemed to appear from thin air. He saw a . . . slice of pizza? And a . . . monster truck? And a . . . giant dragon? Suddenly, there was a voice.

Turbo blinked. Could it be? Was it really who he thought it was? "Leo?"

Leo helped Turbo up from the rock he had been lying on. "Are you okay?" Leo asked. "You sat down and . . . I don't know . . . spaced out."

"Yeah," said Turbo, wiping his forehead with a paw. "It's really hot here."

Turbo looked around. Now he remembered! He had been visiting his friend Leo in Classroom A. But while Turbo's home in Classroom C was a cozy cage filled with cedar chips and a water bottle, Leo's was a desert-like terrarium.

Leo was an official classroom pet. But like Turbo, Leo was not *just* a classroom pet. Turbo and Leo were both secretly superheroes!

But more on that later.

"Maybe we should get you a drink," said Leo.

Leo took Turbo to a small pool of water that looked like it had been carved out of rock. After a few gulps, Turbo felt much more like himself again.

"You have a really nice place, Leo," he said. "But I'm not sure it's quite right for me."

"I'll say." Leo laughed. "You fuzzy guys can't take the heat!"

Suddenly Leo leaped to his feet. "Did you hear that?"

TAP! TAP! TAP!

"It's the Superpet Superhero League alarm!" exclaimed Turbo. "And three taps means there's a super emergency!"

Wait, what's that you say? You've never heard of the Superpet Super-hero League?! Why, the Superpet Superhero League is only the best team of superpets in Sunnyview Elementary history!

Turbo and Leo quickly sprang into action. Within moments, they had transformed into . . .

FISH OUT OF WATER!

Super Turbo and the Great Gecko popped the cover off the vent in Classroom A. The vent system connected all the classrooms in Sunnyview Elementary.

The superpets listened closely to the sound of the taps.

SOFT, WITH A LITTLE BOUNCE TO THE END.

A PENCIL ERASER!

Every member of the Superpet Superhero League used a different tool to tap for help. Turbo, for example, used a ruler. Since this pet was tapping with a pencil, that meant it was Clever!

Clever was a green parakeet, and she was the official pet of Classroom D. She was also a member of the Superpet Superhero League, where

she fought evil as the Green Winger.

Super Turbo followed the Great Gecko down the vent system leading to Classroom D. As they rounded a corner, they bumped into the other members of the Superpet Superhero League.

FRANK

ALIAS: BOSS BUNNY
CLASSROOM: PRINCIPAL'S OFFICE. YEAH, IT'S NOT REALLY A CLASSROOM. FRANK IS THE PERSONAL PET OF PRINCIPAL BAXTER BRICKFORD!
SUPERHERO SKILLS: HIS UTILITY BELT HAS A GADGET FOR ANY OCCASION! AND HE CAN SMELL DANGER!

WARREN

ALIAS: PROFESSOR TURTLE
CLASSROOM: THE SCIENCE LAB
SUPERHERO SKILLS: BEING A TURTLE, HE'S PRETTY SLOW, BUT HE'S ALSO SUPER SMART. ESPECIALLY WHEN IT COMES TO SCIENCE!

The Superpet Superhero League burst out of the vent that led into Classroom D. And there was the Green Winger, perched in her cage. As expected, she was frantic.

"Guys! Thank goodness you're here! Come quick!" she cried. She flew down to the floor of Classroom D and gestured for the other animals to follow her.

As Turbo scurried
along, he nearly
slipped in
something
slick.

"Why is
the floor
all wet?"
he asked.

"That's why!" the Green Winger said, and pointed at something flapping on the ground.

It was Nell!

Nell lay on her side. Next to her was an almost-totally-empty Turbomobile.

"Hi, guys," Nell gasped. "A little help here?"

The Turbomobile had once been an ordinary hamster ball until the Superpet Superhero League had turned it into a way for Fantastic Fish to get around. It had allowed the fish to fight in many memorable battles with evil. But now it had apparently sprung a leak.

"Wonder Pig . . . ,"
began Professor Turtle. "Can you
help me take the Turbomobile . . . to
my lab? I want to . . . go over it and . . .
fix any leaks."

"That's a great idea, Professor
Turtle," said the Great Gecko. "With
your scientific know-how, I'm sure
you'll have the Turbomobile in bet-
ter shape than ever! In the mean-
time, tomorrow is our regularly

scheduled Superpet Superhero League meeting. Let's all get some well-earned rest before then."

"It *has* been a long night!" agreed Super Turbo.

And he meant it. As he headed back to Classroom C, he could barely keep his eyes open. Once he was in his cage, Turbo tucked away his superhero gear and fell fast asleep.

THE SUPERPET SUPERHERO LEAGUE GOES GLOBAL!

Turbo woke up early the next morning. He had slept deeply after his adventure in the desert—or, well, in Leo's terrarium—and after his hard work helping Nell.

RING-A-DING-DING!

The classroom bell! That meant school was starting. Since the students of Classroom C had no idea that their beloved class pet was actually a superhero, it was time for Turbo to act like a normal *non*-super hamster. The second-grade students and their teacher filed in.

Turbo ran a few laps on his wheel.

He ate a few hamster pellets.

He drank from his water bottle.

That should do it, thought Turbo, wiping his mouth with the back of his paw. Secret's still safe!

Ms. Beasley, the teacher, began to address the class. Turbo settled into his favorite listening spot next to his food dish. He used to pay no attention to what the teacher told the students of Classroom C, but Turbo had recently discovered that if he *did*

pay attention, he might actually learn something. As in: *learn* about *something* that might require a superhero to step in and save the day.

"Kids, I have exciting news," said Ms. Beasley. "For the next couple of weeks, the whole school is going to be participating in a very special project!"

Turbo's ears perked up. A special project sounded like superhero business.

"And that special project is . . .
Celebrate the World Day!" Ms.
Beasley announced.

"What's Celebrate the World
Day?" asked a student.

"Good question, Sally," replied
Ms. Beasley. "Leading up to the
event, each class at Sunnyview Elementary will research and study
one country. Then, the day of, the
classes will celebrate the country
they've studied! We'll decorate our
classrooms, dress in traditional
clothing, and serve traditional food.
We'll travel around the world by

going from class to class, and we'll learn all about different countries!"

Wow, thought Turbo. *That sounds pretty cool! Maybe we superpets don't need to step in after all.*

Ms. Beasley proceeded to announce which country each classroom would be celebrating.

Turbo listened excitedly. Wow! The whole Superpet Superhero league was involved. But something was missing. There was one pet left out. Turbo couldn't think of who it was. But then . . .

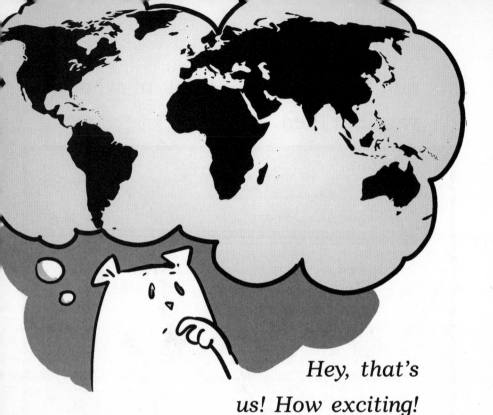

Hey, that's us! How exciting! thought Turbo. *But . . . where's Japan?*

Oh well, he'd have a lot of time to learn. Turbo couldn't wait until the pets' team meeting tonight so they could gush over this exciting new project. The Superpet Superhero League was going global!

Meanwhile, through a small crack in the wall near Classroom C's book nook, a pair of beady eyes were gleaming.

CELEBRATE THE WORLD DAY? MORE LIKE TAKE OVER THE WORLD DAY!

FUN FACTS AND RAT PACKS

That night, all the animals were
holding their Superpet Superhero
League meeting in the hallway of
Sunnyview Elementary. This way,
Nell could attend. Professor Turtle
was still working on fixing the
Turbomobile.

On the way to the meeting, Turbo

and Angelina had stopped by the library to pick up some books, and the animals were eagerly reading up on their classrooms' countries.

The upcoming Celebrate the World Day was very exciting. So exciting, in fact, that the superpets had pretty much forgotten to be super. Instead they just traded cool facts about their countries with one another.

The superpets were so wrapped up in all these cool new facts that they didn't notice a couple of small fuzzy animals watching them from around the corner. The two animals whispered to each other and disappeared through a hole in the wall.

If the superpets *had* been paying attention, they might have seen these fuzzy creatures, followed them, and discovered that they went skittering through the walls, down the halls, and into the cafeteria, where they then joined a huge crowd of other fuzzy creatures. It was . . .

THE RAT PACK!

And in the middle of the pack, standing on a stale bagel, was . . .

WHISKERFACE!

Whiskerface was a tiny rat with huge ears who was just about as evil as they come.

"I need a report on our plans for sabotage!" he bellowed. "Starting with Classroom A!"

Two rats stepped forward. "The kindergarteners of Classroom A will be celebrating Brazil," said one of them. "The most popular sport in Brazil is soccer."

"*Futbol*," corrected the other rat. "They call it *futbol*."

"Yeah, yeah. They're building a miniature *futbol* stadium. We're going to chew through the supports of their tiny stands, and smash it all with a soccer ball attack!"

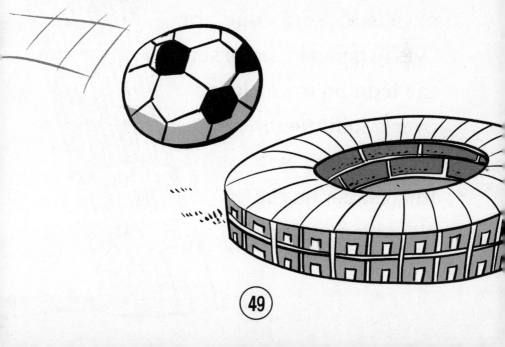

"Excellent!" said Whiskerface, rubbing his little paws together. "Classroom B! Report!"

Two more rats came forward. "The first-grade students of Classroom B are making their own Leaning Tower of Pisa," said one rat. "We're going to make sure the leaning tower leans over a liiiiiittle too far!"

"Then it will fall, smashing the classroom as flat

as a pizza!" said the other.

Whiskerface laughed his squeaky high-pitched laugh. "Classroom C!"

"The highest point in Japan is Mount Fuji. It's a volcano! The students are making a model," said a rat.

"We're going to make that volcano erupt!" cried his companion nastily.

"Yes! Yes!" shouted Whiskerface, clapping. "Classroom D!"

"Classroom D is Kenya!" another rat announced. "The Third graders are making giant models of safari animals. We will sneak our agents *into* the giraffe model. Bet those kids didn't think a cardboard giraffe could actually walk!"

Whiskerface cackled with delight. "What else do we have?"

"The science lab is going to be Switzerland. They are recreating Lake Geneva. And we're going to make sure that lake overflows!"

"The principal's office will be Russia. They're going to be making borscht." The rat who spoke shuddered with disgust. "Borscht is a cold beet soup. And it's gross. So we kind of figure that's already ruined," he said.

"And, finally," said one rat, as he walked forward, "the hallways are China. In ancient times, China was connected to the rest of the world by trade routes called the Silk Road. The students are turning the hallways into a modern Silk Road."

"But!" said another rat, smiling. "We're going to block the hallways with our very own Great Wall of China! Everyone will be trapped in their classrooms!"

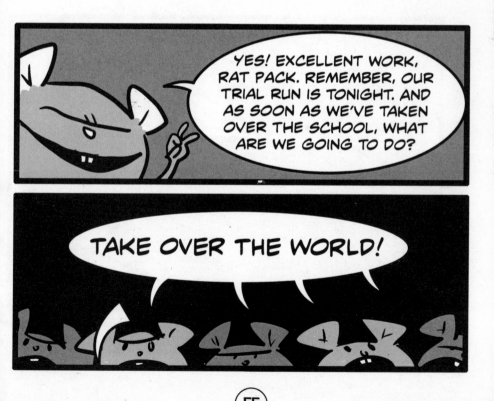

5

NIGHTTIME NOISES

Turbo was snug as a bug in his hamster cage when he heard it. He wasn't sure what it was, but he knew it was *something*. The last time Turbo woke up to a strange sound in the middle of the night, he ended up having to battle the evil Pencil Pointer.

He listened as hard as he could with his little hamster ears. He thought he could make out the sound of . . . squeaking?

"Hello? Is anyone there?" Turbo called out.

The squeaking stopped. Well, that was suspicious.

SURELY THIS IS A JOB FOR . . . SUPER TURBO!

Using his super-
hamster agility, Super
Turbo snuck out of
his cage and quietly
scampered across
the classroom to
Ms. Beasley's desk.
That's where the
squeaking seemed to
be coming from.

Super Turbo discovered that the
bottom desk drawer was wide open.
Then he looked up and saw that
the other desk drawers had been
opened, too, but only partway.

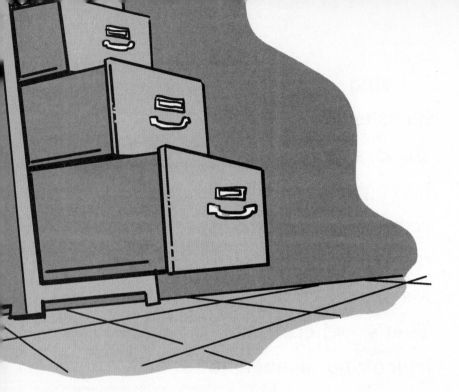

Looks oddly like a staircase, Super Turbo thought. *And what would Super Turbo do? He'd climb that staircase!*

The only problem was . . . even *Super* Turbo was still pretty small.

He took a running start and . . .
SMACK! He bounced off the bottom
drawer.

That was all the boost he needed. Super Turbo climbed up the drawer-stairs to the top of Ms. Beasley's desk and was face-to-face with . . . no one.

Whoever had opened the drawers, whoever had been here, whoever had been *squeaking*, had left.

From where he now stood on top of Ms. Beasley's desk, Super Turbo realized that he had a perfect view of the whole class and all its decorations!

THE TEA SET OVER
BY THE BOOK NOOK

THE MODEL OF MOUNT
FUJI OVER BY THAT
CRACK IN THE WALL

Super Turbo admired all the hard work the kids of Classroom C had put into Celebrate the World Day. More than ever, he felt that he needed to keep a watchful eye over the classroom.

Suddenly, he heard another noise. But this time, it was different.

The Superpet Superhero Alarm! But which superpet was tapping?

TAP! TAP! TAP!

Super Turbo concentrated. The taps were sort of hard and sort of waxy? It was a crayon! That meant he needed to get to Classroom A immediately! The Great Gecko was in trouble!

AROUND THE WORLD IN TWENTY MINUTES

All of the superpets had gathered in Classroom A, except for Fantastic Fish, who was still stuck in her tank.

"Just putting a few touches on the Turbomobile," explained Professor Turtle.

The animals were huddled around the Great Gecko, who was staring at a giant piece of paper that lay on the floor. It was slightly torn and a little crumpled.

"Just look at it!" he said sadly. "It's ruined!'

"I'll say!" said Boss Bunny. "It looks like it was painted by a bunch of five-year-olds."

"That's because it *was* painted by a bunch of five-year-olds!" cried the Great Gecko. "This was the banner my kids made to celebrate their country, Brazil! They worked so hard on it. And now it's destroyed!"

"Uh, guys," said Wonder Pig. "If Whiskerface and his Rat Pack are still out there. And we're all in here—"

"Then who's protecting our class-rooms?!" cried the Green Winger.

"I think . . . it will be faster . . . if we split up . . . and each go to . . . our own rooms," said Professor Turtle, as quickly as he possibly could. He looked around. The other superpets had already run off. "Oh . . . never mind, then."

The superpets raced through the vents and arrived at Classroom B, Wonder Pig's home.

"Oh no!" Wonder Pig shouted. "The Leaning Tower of

Pisa looks like it's leaning a liiiittle too much!"

Boss Bunny sniffed the air. "I think they've already left! Let's go to the next class!"

The superpets ran to Classroom D, home base of the Green Winger. Just as they arrived, a loud *CRASH* rang out.

"Oh no!" exclaimed the Green Winger. "They just spilled these beads all over the floor! My kids had been sorting these for days!"

The superpets ran back to the vent and hurried to the science lab. They arrived seconds after Professor Turtle, who had gone straight there at his usual turtle speed. Everything was covered in what looked like snow!

Boss Bunny sniffed the air. "It smells so clean!" he cried with delight.

"That's because . . . these are flakes of . . . *soap*," concluded Professor Turtle. "It's a . . . soapy avalanche!" he said, looking around in horror.

Once again, the superpets were already racing out the door.

"Superpets!" shouted Nell from her aquarium in the hallway. "I just saw them! They ran under the door to the principal's office! If you hurry, you can catch them!"

That did it for Boss Bunny.

No one messed with Principal Brickford's office!

With a mighty bunny hop, Boss Bunny hurled himself at the mail slot in the door of the principal's office.

And the superpets did hurry, but by the time they got the door open, the Rat Pack was long gone.

Fortunately, it looked like they hadn't done any damage there.

But they sure had done a lot to the rest of the school. And it was up to the superpets to fix this mess before the students and teachers arrived the next morning.

It was going to be a long, long night.

7

TODAY'S THE DAY!

It had taken the superpets all night and even into the early morning to clean up the ugly worldwide mess. Then they had spent the rest of the week looking for the Rat Pack in the cafeteria, but Whiskerface and his evil minions were nowhere to be found.

Turbo was in his cage in Class-room C, pacing back and forth. Today was the big one. Today was Celebrate the World Day. If the Rat Pack was going to pull some dirty move, it was going to happen *now*.

Turbo was sure that they were planning something *truly* evil.

Suddenly Turbo noticed that one of his students was staring at him. Pacing back and forth wasn't exactly normal hamster behavior, so he

quickly ran over to his hamster wheel and began running on it.

To be fair, Turbo wasn't looking very *normal* right now anyway.

As part of Celebrate the World Day, some students had dressed Turbo in a hamster-sized traditional Japanese outfit. Turbo thought it looked pretty cool, though it didn't really leave room for his cape.

Turbo glanced at the clock. Soon, the students of Classroom C, along with the rest of Sunnyview Elementary, would head to the school cafeteria. That was where they were having the great feast with food from around the world.

The Superpet Superhero League had decided that as soon as all the kids left their classrooms, the pets would gather for an emergency meeting.

It was risky business. They had never met during school hours before, but they had never faced such a threat before either! Whatever Whiskerface and his Rat Pack were up to, they had to be stopped!

And the Superpet Superhero League was the school's only defense.

RING-A-DING-DING!

The lunch bell rang, and the students of Classroom C filed out of the classroom. Turbo slipped from his cage, crawled down the table, and made his way to the vent. He managed to awkwardly tuck his cape into his kimono.

He scurried through the vents to the meeting place: below the aquarium in the hallway. When Super Turbo arrived, he gasped.

WOW, LOOK AT YOU GUYS!

Suddenly, a squeaky voice rang out behind the superpets. "Well, I think you look like a bunch of ninnies!"

It was Whiskerface! And his Rat Pack!

PROTECTING THE SCHOOL—AND THE WORLD!

Whiskerface paced back and forth, gleefully rubbing his paws together. "Do you know why today is a great day? Not only am I going to defeat the superpests—I'm going to ruin Celebrate the World Day, and then I'm going to take over the *actual* world!" he cackled.

"We're *not* going to let you ruin Celebrate the World Day!" cried Turbo.

"Oh really?" said Whiskerface with a sneer. "Well, guess what? You're too late!"

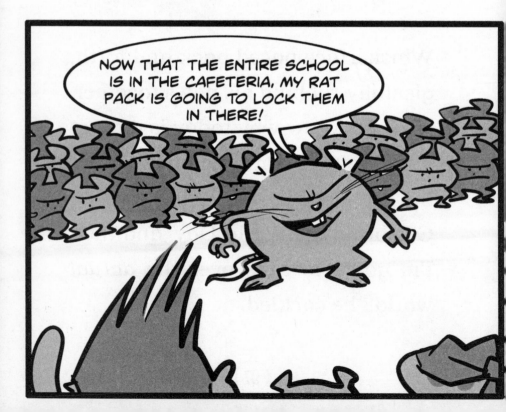

Whiskerface snapped his fingers. On cue, the Rat Pack swarmed the hallway. They linked arms to form a rather disgusting-looking chain of rats, completely blocking the hall.

The Rat Pack advanced on the superpets. On the other side of the wall, Turbo saw that a second group of rats was creating a tower by standing on top of one another so that they could lock the cafeteria door. If they reached that lock, they really *would* trap the entire school!

"We've got to stop them!" cried Turbo. But how?!

Suddenly, a loud rumbling sound filled the hallway.

"I *still* say you left a few steps out of that plan of yours!" yelled Fantastic Fish. She was in the new-and-improved Turbomobile. And riding on top was Boss Bunny!

9

THE FANTASTICALLY FISHY PLAN!

The Fantastic Fish Tank burst through the great wall of rats, scattering them like bowling pins. Boss Bunny hopped off the back, joining his friends.

"Sorry we're late," he apologized.

"Actually, I'd say you guys were right on time!" cried Super Turbo.

Meanwhile, Fantastic Fish spun down the hallway in her Fantastic Fish Tank. She smacked into the tower of rats.

"What are you doing?!" screamed Whiskerface to his Rat Pack. All the rats were walking around a bit dazed. "Get that talking fish!" he shrieked.

But Fantastic Fish was a few steps ahead of the evil rat. She steered the Fantastic Fish Tank at full speed right for her aquarium.

The Superpet Superhero League stared at her, afraid of what was about to happen.

At the last second, Fantastic Fish unlatched the top of the Fantastic Fish Tank. Then she leaped out. And just in the nick time!

Whiskerface and the Rat Packers were soaked. If there's anything rats hate more than loud noises and superpets, it's being wet. Crying like babies, Whiskerface and his Rat Pack scampered down the hallway.

The superpets ran over to Fantastic Fish, who lay flopping in a shallow puddle.

"Oh no!" cried the Green Winger. "Not again!"

"Get back to your classrooms," gasped Fantastic Fish. "Turbo, hide the new Fantastic Fish Tank. Oh, I also renamed the Turbomobile. Is that okay?"

"Of course it is!" said Super Turbo. "But we can't leave you here!"

"Listen, I'll be fine," Fantastic Fish said. "With the commotion we created, people are going to come running. Any second now, someone will help me."

"Now, that's what I call a hero!" said the Great Gecko.

"Guys . . . we've got . . . to go. I hear someone . . . coming," said Professor Turtle.

The rest of the superpets heard it too. With a last glance at Fantastic Fish, Super Turbo and the others raced away just as Ms. Beasley and a crowd of students burst from the cafeteria.

 **10**

SAFE AND SOUND

A little while later, Turbo sat in his comfy cage, munching on some seaweed and edamame. What a day it had been! The Superpet Superhero League had faced perhaps their greatest challenge yet, and they had won! And to top it off, they had even kept their secret identities safe.

Turbo turned to look at the glass jar next to him on the shelf.

"Care for some edamame?" he asked Nell.

After the commotion in the hallway, Ms. Beasley had been the first to find Nell. She'd taken Nell back to Classroom C and put her safely

inside a jar of water, just until her aquarium could be replaced.

"No, thanks," Nell replied. "I'm more of a dried worm kind of gal."

The students of Classroom C were busy presenting all they knew about Japan to students from other classes.

They would never know how close
Celebrate the World Day had come
to being ruined, but that didn't mat-
ter. Turbo was just glad that Whiskerface had been stopped . . . this time.
Surely there would be another time

when the school—and the world—
needed protecting. And when that
time came . . .

THE SUPERPET SUPERHERO LEAGUE
WOULD BE THERE!

MI-TEE!

Visit
CaptainAwesomeBooks.com
for completely awesome
activities, excerpts,
tips from Turbo, and
the series trailer!